The People in the Desert Town

Written and illustrated by:

Barbara Steele Broome Warlick

Copyright © 2023 Barbara Steele Broome Warlick

All rights reserved.

ISBN: 9798851308499

This book is a work of fiction. Names, characters, places, and incidents are used fictitiously -from the author's imagination. Anything similar to actual people, organizations, towns, or events is coincidental.

DEDICATION

I want to dedicate this book in memory of my time spent in Texas. I got to see desert flowers and animals. I heard coyotes and saw jack rabbits. I am thankful for the time I got to spend with my husband and two boys in Texas. I got to see pipes that ran water from New Mexico down to El Paso, Texas.

I also want to dedicate this book to my husband Howard who likes my cactus garden.

Acknowledgement

I want to thank God for the idea for this book in a dream.

There was an old man and woman in their eighties, named Ted and Lily Simpson who wanted to get a land grant near the end of the desert. It was near Mountain Town, Texas. They came by wagon train from Valley, Texas. The wagon train stopped in the Texas R Town in Flag, Texas. They bought supplies with plenty of seeds. Why they bought the seeds, no one knew. They went to the depot.
    Ben sent a telegram to the governor's office and asked for a land grant for Mr. and Mrs. Simpson for land in the far part of the desert, near the Mountain Town. Ben told them that it might not get approved, but the reply came back from the governor that it was approved. They thanked Ben and told him to call them Ted and Lily. Ted and Lily told Ben they had always wanted to live in a desert, and they were so happy it was approved. Their wish had finally come true.
    The wagon train finally reached the Mountain Town. Ted and Lily paid to have a pipe that would carry water from the Mountain Town spring to the back of their large one room cabin. They also ordered a well pump. They hired some men to hook it all up for them.
    They bought their logs and windowpanes to make a cabin and a barn. They wanted to buy horses and a milk cow. All other foods would be bought from the railhead near Mountain Town. They didn't want to grow anything, but they planned to cultivate what was already growing there. They would have to plant wheat seeds to grow wheat for the animals.

Ted and Lily got everything built. They really liked their cabin. The Simpson's had a little dog named Jewel that they brought with them.

The barn was ready for the cow and horses.

Ted and Lily started on their flower garden. They planted their desert flowers.

They planted desert plants and cacti.

The Simpsons planned to make cactus candy and jelly to sell in the Mountain Town. People did not understand why they wanted to live in the desert. Ted and Lily told the people that they loved the desert. They wanted to make friends with the animals by feeding and watering them.

The Simpson's had a son, named Shawn, and a daughter named Emma. Shawn was married to Rebecca and Emma was married to Ronnie. The couples planned to join Ted and Lily in the summer. The desert seemed to be a neglected place, but it could be a wonderful place to live.

Ted and Lily's children got their land grant approved. Ted and Lily registered their town as the Desert Town. The wild animals were curious about the cabin and barn. They saw the water pan and the seed pan. They finally began to eat the seeds and drink the water.

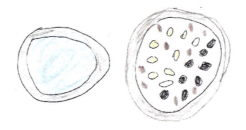

The Simpsons were afraid of some animals. There was a bobcat that chased Jewel from the barn all the way back to the front of the cabin. Jewel ran onto the steps. Lily saw her and grabbed her and said, "Get in here, quick!" Lily slammed the door on the growling bobcat.

Ted found out that the bobcat had been living in the barn and scaring the cow and horses. Jewel just happened to come in the barn and that's when the bobcat saw her.

The bobcat had babies in the barn loft. Before they got too big, Ted would take them to the forest near Mountain Town and let them go.

The animals finally found the food and water the Simpsons put out for them. They had rats, jackrabbits, coyote, sand grouse, cactus wren, and a pygmy owl. It was a wonderful sight, seeing all the animals.

They even learned there was a sand cat in the desert. It came to eat and drink. Lily even made corn cakes for the animals. The animals seemed to love it.

Ted and Lily made lots of photo shots of the animals and the gardens. They developed them in their dark room. They sent some pictures to the newspaper in the Texas R Town. The newspaper paid them for the photos and stories that Lily wrote. People were eager to learn about the desert and about Ted and Lily Simpson's life there.

A wagon train came to the Mountain Town. Ted and Lily's son and daughter and their spouses were on the wagon train. Their son Shawn rented a buggy to use to travel to the desert property.

They were happy to get started on their cabin and barn. They loved the garden their parents had made. They went back to the Mountain Town and hired some men to bring logs for the cabins and barns.

Ted and Lily told their children to come and give them a hug. Emma had already told her parents that they all needed a new start. Ted and Lily told their children that they had named it the Desert Town. They all laughed and told their parents that was a pretty good, natural name. Ted and Lily talked about Jewel and the incident she had with the bobcat. They told their children that the animals were getting tamer.

The children were going to stay in their covered wagon until their barns and cabins were built.

Rebecca   Shawn

Ted told the children that there were many night animals, and they could hear an owl at night. They looked out the window and saw a Dama Deer and a bat.

In the daytime, a sand lizard came out, a scorpion, bobcat, and even a rattlesnake. When it got hot, they would go to where it was cooler, some in burrows.

   The children thought they were feeding some dangerous animals. They didn't realize how many animals were in the desert. Lily told them that the cutest one was the sand cat that looked about the same as their cats, except their heads were bigger and their bodies were longer than the cats they knew. The children had never heard of such a thing. Lily told them that she cooked corn cakes for the sand cats and they loved it.

   The men were discussing the barn and cabin when they heard Emma scream. She had gone into the barn to get the eggs for her mom.

The men looked up and the bobcat was chasing Emma. Emma made it back to the cabin safely.

The men were out back of the cabin discussing the barns and cabins again, when they heard Rebecca screaming. They all ran around to the front of the cabin, and Rebecca had almost stepped on a rattlesnake, who was getting water from the pan that Lily had just put out.

Ted took the wagon and went to the Mountain Town and bought apples to can and to feed the animals.

The next day, Lily and the women canned apple jelly and applesauce. The women also made cactus jelly and cactus candy. Lily planned to sell some at the Mountain Town and ship some to other towns.

They finally got the cabins and barns built. They got water piped to all of the cabins and pumps put in. There were many people, because of the photos sent to the paper, that came out to see the Desert Town.

Ted and Lily and their children decided to build some small cabins on some of the land for tourists to spend a week in the Desert Town. The tourists would stop at the Mountain Town and rent a wagon to bring them out to the Desert Town. The money that they made from renting the cabins gave Ted and Lily, and their children a good income.

They had plenty of candy and jelly for the tourists to buy. Lily had a good idea and told the rest of her family about it. Her idea was to make dish towels and other items with the animals embroidered on them. That would be another good attraction for the tourists.

The men decided to do their part, so they built a workshop where they could carve little animals, boxes, and other things.

One night, before they put their animals in the barn, Lily and her family heard a terrible noise. They all looked out the window and saw a black bear fighting with the bobcat. The bear soon ran off after the bobcat clawed it on the nose.

Everything was built and furnished, even the tourist cabins. Lily and her family were ready for their first tourist. A letter was sent to the newspaper in the Texas R Town telling how the Desert Town was ready for tourists. Only three parties at a time could visit the Desert Town, but there would be a waiting list. The tourists would make reservations at the Mountain Town by writing a letter.

They soon had their first tourist, and everything went well. The tourist had two boys and they called Jewel a "Meow, Meow," but Jewel was a dog.

Lily and her family decided to have a picnic to celebrate their life in the desert town. The picnic was a success, and the food was delicious. A lot of the food was made from plants and cactus out of Lily's garden.

They bought greens and mushrooms from the Mountain Town. They had a mild winter and a light snow. It stayed sixty degrees about all winter.

Lily got her family together again and said she had another idea. They all wanted to know what it was. Lily told them that they had been taking a lot of pictures and had learned a lot about the animals and the plant life there, in the desert. She told them they needed to write a book and could even do some children's books. The children told her it was a wonderful idea and they got started right away with it. When they finished, they sent their manuscripts off to be published. They soon had books to sell.

They were getting so many animals in the Desert Town, that even the fearless raccoon was scared of some of them. They had too many rattlesnakes and they were scaring everyone.

Emma got slightly bit by a rattlesnake. She had to be rushed to the doctor in the Mountain Town. They gave her a shot of anti-venom. The doctor told her she would need plenty of rest for a few weeks.

There were some men in the Mountain Town that caught rattlesnakes. The snakes were milked, and the anti-venom was made. Ted got the men to come to the Desert Town to catch the rattlesnakes. They would be free of them for a while.

One day, Jewel got in a fight with a sand cat. The cat clawed her pretty badly, so Ted and Lily took her to a vet in the Mountain Town. The vet told them that Jewel would be alright and would soon be her old self again.

The children thought Lily should stop feeding the animals for a while, but Lily did not agree with that. Even with all the dangerous animals, the Desert Town was a wonderful place to be.

Ted and Lily and their family still loved the Desert Town and planned to stay. The animals would just have to be monitored but they would manage. The town was all that they had hoped it would be. Ted and Lily were very happy. The books and all the things they made to sell was a great success. Now, people would read their books and know that the Desert Town was a special place.

Ted and Lily had one final surprise. They found out that Emma and Rebecca were both expecting a baby in the summer, only a few months away. They were all so happy in the Desert Town in Texas.

Made in the USA
Middletown, DE
16 July 2023